Tender Hoof

Stories

Nicole Rivas

Thirty West Publishing House

Contents

Tender Hoof

Demolished

THERE WAS A GRAY-HAIRED MAN who lived in the house across the street, the burnt one being torn down. He lived there with his elderly parents. I never saw much of the parents, but I often saw the man. I saw his shirtless body reclined on a pool chair in his otherwise empty garage. His stomach always seemed to be damp and sprawling past the outskirts of his form, and from my vantage point in the street it looked like he was lying on a gurney. Only his occasional bodily shifts suggested that he wasn't actually dead.

In the beginning, I rollerbladed past the open garage and wondered why he didn't just go to the nearby pool. He was belly-up on the pool chair, sweating. Over dinner, my parents gossiped amongst themselves, unaware that I was also interested in the neighbor's story. According to them, the man worked at a fast food restaurant during the evenings. He had been married once, no kids. He even owned a restaurant. Then a divorce and now, at age forty-eight, back at home. "How sad," my parents agreed.

Eventually, a teenager claimed the man beckoned her into his garage and tried to lick her neck. What an odd thing to attempt. The adults didn't know what to believe; the girl smoked pot and was known to vandalize street signs. And the gray-haired man with his bare chest, just what was he trying to communicate? Finally, my parents spoke to me directly about the neighbor. It seemed they thought they were bringing him to my attention. "Don't rollerblade that way anymore," they said. "And if anything, weird happens, tell us."

Soon, the man stopped sitting with the garage door open. It was as if he had shouted, "I don't want to see anyone's neck, let alone lick it."

The day the house caught fire, I was at school learning about The Donner Party. About the poor decisions, the cannibalism. There didn't seem to be a moral to the story, only the observation that humans make terrible mistakes and that no one ever forgets them. After school, I rollerbladed past an empty garage that looked like a giant, burnt oven. The man had placed a towel on the hot stove, laid on the pool chair, and fallen asleep. The elderly parents were fine, but the gray-haired man was not.

Now, everyone blames the teenager for the man's death. They no longer believe her and her neck-licking story. They think she is the kind of girl who would want her neck licked. They think many things that they didn't before. They think the man was a great help to his parents, if not a little shy, or depressed, but maybe also a saint, his head crowned in golden ash, the kind hard to see in passing.

The Boy with Chambered Nautiluses for Hair

THE PRIEST LIED WHEN HE SAID that he didn't know the boy personally, even when the boy described a birthmark on the priest's inner thigh which resembled a shark's tooth. After that he continued to lie, even when his ex-wife corroborated the birthmark detail.

Lots of people have birthmarks, the priest said.

This was true.

My body is not a Rorschach, the priest said, pounding the table in front of him.

Technically, this was also true. His body was not a Rorschach. His body was a body.

The boy was eleven years old with black hair that curled around his ears and looked like the inner shells of chambered nautiluses. His parents had died over the summer in a car accident while on their way home from the grocery store. A drunk woman driving the wrong way. Everyone dead on impact. For a week, the freeway was littered with his parents' smashed mangoes, reusable bags, and the blood red of shattered tail lights. At the time, the boy was playing at a friend's house. That evening, his mother was going to surprise the boy with ripe mangoes sliced in half moons and dusted in red chili powder, lime juice, and salt. Instead, all that remained was a roadside memorial, two metal crosses sticking out of the body of the earth like ingrown hairs.

Time passed. The priest was briefly questioned, let go. The boy with chambered nautiluses for hair was quietly swept up to live with his grandparents several hours away. His grief would be a silent grief, something relegated to a dusty corner of the house and turned sour over time. When the priest returned to the school the following week, the boys looked at each other, and then at the empty seat of the boy with chambered nautiluses for hair. Where had he gone? No one had an answer, at least not for them. The priest began his sermon on the virtues of honesty. Pick up your pencils, take notes. With each word he spoke, someone's heaven shattered. The boys held their breaths, erasers pointed towards a heavy sky, and waited for the shards.

Don't Mention It

THE BICYCLIST IS ACCUSTOMED to getting yelled at by men in moving vehicles. Hackneyed phrases like, "Hey, baby," and "Juicy ass," and "How much for an hour?" Tonight, a blur of a man in a blue compact car whizzes by her in the opposite direction. "Give me that pussy!" Faceless. The bicyclist pedals onward. One mile elapses. When she steers into the gravel alleyway behind her apartment complex, she is thinking about the jarred okra sitting in the refrigerator upstairs. Her mouth waters at the thought of fat seeds dripping brine, a private feast standing over the kitchen sink, sweat soaking through the back of her t-shirt.

She dismounts her bicycle and removes her helmet. "Hey, baby!" The bicyclist turns around and sees the familiar blue compact car, the man hunched over the steering wheel within it. He follows her home. A cigarette dangles from his hand, which she only knows because the smoke catches in the alleyway's one lamp. Without thinking, she picks up her bicycle and hoists it above her head, as if the man were a mountain lion who might be deterred by her superficial size. But even then, she is too scared to say anything. Her helmet topples onto the ground. The man smirks at her display, presses the cigarette to his lips, and drives away.

The bicyclist hauls her bicycle into her apartment, occasionally looking over her shoulder. The alleyway is empty and the gravel glitters in the moonlight. Once inside the apartment, she locks the door, closes the curtains. She lifts her bicycle onto its rack, pauses. She returns to the door, draws open the curtains to peer outside. The alleyway hasn't changed. She makes sure the door is locked again and briefly wishes for a padlock. She takes the bicycle off its rack and leans it in front of the door. Barriers. Alarm systems. She goes to take a shower. Takes the kitchen knife with her. Undresses in the tub. The ribbons of stripped clothing give her the feeling of being slowly and irrevocably whittled away.

Once in bed, she gets as comfortable as possible before getting out of bed to make sure her bedroom door is locked again. A hammer rests beneath her pillow. It was her father's. She calls her mother in Florida but it's late and her mother doesn't answer. The bicyclist leaves a cheery message but doesn't say anything about the man who followed her home. Too embarrassed or something. She thinks about the summer she turned fourteen and the neighbor, Mr. Barry, invited her over for popsicles. The whole thing became a weekly ritual. Suck a popsicle, suck my finger. Suck a popsicle, suck my dick. Suck a popsicle while I take a photo of you looking coy but really just imitating coyness to hide the overflowing shame. Suck a popsicle and don't tell anyone about this or they'll think you're a slut. A slut who loves to suck.

It was a mistake to tell them, the bicyclist thinks. Her parents. She touches the hammer's head and is shocked by its coldness. Mom and dad didn't really want to hear about the neighbor. That's why nobody ever mentioned it again. Nobody wanted another fault. And then dad died. So, really. Don't mention it.

As the bicyclist falls asleep, she forgets about the pickled okra which she had nearly dreamt about an hour or so ago. Where did that desire go? That growing promise? The hunger is gone, suspended somewhere out of the bicyclist's reach. No dinner tonight, just a feast of outdoor sounds that make the bicyclist's chest ache. The sounds will turn into nightmares. But nightmares end, at least sometimes.

The Invention of Father

When they invented our father, it was to punish us. We had been doing just fine without one. They said our father would have door knobs for knuckles, that he would be born old. They said he would kiss us without warning, take photos of us doing our math homework because he never made it very far in school and our ability to perform long division amazed him. They said his salt-and-pepper stubble would rub our cheeks raw.

They said our father would have hobbies that we wouldn't be able to relate to. In the Spring, he would walk out on our porch and shoot the nesting house sparrows with a small, dull gun. We would cry about such violence, and he would put one heavy hand on our shoulder and tell us to get the dustpan from inside. We would retrieve the dustpan as told and wordlessly watch him collect the sparrow corpses and their stray, blood-flecked feathers.

We would be secretly embarrassed because even though we hated guns, we wished his was shinier, that it looked more threatening in his rough-hewn hand. At least when our friends were over. We wanted him to know more things than he did, the right things and in the right way. We would wish his care was a different kind of care.

As he continued to grow older, they said another favorite hobby of father's would be to drag us to the restaurant deep in the woods, to say the strange and embarrassing things to waitstaff that seemed to make them uncomfortable and make us hang our blushing faces over our root vegetable stew. Eventually we would go to the restaurant deep in the woods every Friday for dinner. In between chews of morel mushroom bisque, our father would flirt with a server who was too young for him, who was barely out of college. Her name was Clementine. He would show Clementine his gold tooth and she would giggle, touching her wolf's tooth earring. Much to our horror, they would be married soon thereafter. But it didn't turn out like we expected, and our stepmother would be too bored in our small house to behave meanly to us. She would hardly look at us at all and wouldn't ask any questions except to inquire if anyone had seen her slippers so she could walk outside and smoke a cigarette.

They said the punishment would hit the hardest in the end. First, they said that we wouldn't even remember what we were being punished for. Then our father would grow too blind to notice the house sparrows, too deaf to hear their calls, and too tired to care. He wouldn't take any more photos of us or suggest dining at the restaurant deep in the woods. They said our stepmother would abandon him in pursuit of something or someone better, that we would be all he had left. They said that one night, when he should have been sleeping, we would walk into his bedroom to find him curled up in a ball and weeping. He would not be able to tell us what year it was. He would not even be able to tell us why he was crying. They said that in this moment we would finally see how small he had been this whole time. They said that once we learned that we loved our father, truly loved him, that he would not even be able to name us.

The Invention of Mother

WHEN BROTHER AND I RAN AWAY from home, brother dropped mother's weight loss pills on the ground in case we changed our minds. The pills were small, rectangular, and a nondescript white, like mother felt she should be. To us, mother always looked gaunt and scared. Sometimes scary. Even when she hunched over to hug us, we recoiled from her gloomy body. Yellow and cold, it reminded us of clothes suspended damp on hangers, or of when we found the old man hanging in the woods by a rope around his throat. Soon thereafter, we learned to wear the same clothes every day without wanting for more.

Brother didn't know why we were running away, so I told him. *We're running away to erase the future. We're running away to invent a new mother.*

Within a day of walking through the forest, we came upon the inventor's home. She lived in a boulder with a door trimmed with quartz. We had never seen anything like it. The door's hinges were marvelous, coffin-shaped pearls the size of our thumbs. We knocked on the inventor's door. She invited us in and showed us a father clock in the foyer that she had fashioned out of a bear corpse. Brother touched its pelt and it winked. This made us feel a certain kind of safety, that a person who could make a clock out of a living, breathing bear could do for us anything we needed. Over steaming dandelion tea, we told the inventor about our mother, about her body and its impending absence.

"I know about your mother," the inventor said at last, leaning back in her chair and sipping the last of her brew. "She comes at the first of every month. I give her a satchel of medicine."

"But you're an inventor," I said, raising an eyebrow. "Not a doctor."

"Your mother wants to reinvent herself. As an inventor, I facilitate that."

Brother choked on his tea. *Facilitate.* Then he studied his chewed up fingernails, listening intently to what the inventor might say next.

"What does 'facilitate' mean?" I interrupted. Brother's ears reddened. It was bad enough that I was the baby sister, but now I had to be the stupid sister, too.

"It's an adult word. It means you don't need a new mother," the inventor said. She patted me on the head, messing up my braids, and allowed us to finish our tea before showing us to the door.

On our way home, we followed the pills that brother had dropped. They gleamed brightly, obviously in an otherwise black-soiled path. Not even the birds had shown interest in them. I felt defeated, but brother was nearly skipping. I guessed he was excited to get home to a warm bath and porridge thick with golden honey. He was excited to get home to the possibility of a mother. *Who*, I thought, *is the stupid one now?*

It wasn't long before we saw the roof of our cottage peeking out from beneath the foliage. Brother began to run up the path toward home. I turned, keeping both feet tight to the ground, waiting. It seemed that the inventor had created something vaguely medicinal for us after all. A cure for boredom and body aches: anticipation so worrisome it made me nauseous.

It was then that we saw mother. She was toward the head of the path, crouching down and gathering the discarded pills in her delicately cupped hand. If I didn't know any better, I would have thought she was gathering berries. She looked up, and when she saw us her first instinct seemed to be to protect the white tablets, to bring them up to the warmth of her chest as if they, and not us, were her precious young. For a moment I felt a sadness sweep over the forest like a shadow. When mother weakly smiled at us, brother stopped dead in his tracks, the only thing skipping: a heart.

Once Upon a Time I Was Someone Else

THE BOY SAYS THAT IN A PAST LIFE, he was a grandfather. He claims he had three grandchildren and that he died of lung cancer, in bed, surrounded by his family. Everyone sitting on folding chairs in the library has read the boy's book and heard this part of the story. The memoir is called, Once Upon a Time I Was Someone Else, and on the book's cover the boy is pictured wearing a tweed blazer with a pipe jutting out of his thin smirk.

Today, the boy is sitting on an armchair in front of us wearing a button-up shirt and slacks. His eyes are a stony gray, and his hair is so blonde it's almost white. It's incredibly fine, his hair. It flutters and flaps in the breeze of the library's overhead fans, like the feathers of a baby bird.

His parents sit on his left, a little too wrinkled and shrunken for the parents of a ten-year-old. They look like they could be siblings.

On the boy's right sits Amanda, my coworker, who told me she believes in everything the boy says. She's read Once Upon a Time I Was Someone Else twice and cried both times.

As Amanda and I were setting up the snack table, she told me that and more. Amanda arranged the paper napkins into a crescent moon. She said that she believes in reincarnation, in the power of the stars, in soulmates, and in the prophetic properties of dreams. In response, I opened the tin of store brand butter cookies with a loud pop, gathered up the crinkly plastic seal, and crushed it into a small ball before throwing it into the trash can.

Everyone is quiet while listening to the boy read from his book, even the children who were dragged here by their parents. The boy closes his eyes and begins. He explains that in his past life, his hair was jet black until his 50s. He says he used to smoke a corn cob pipe and that his name was Henry Owens. Everyone already knows this, but they still lean forward to listen, slack-jawed in the face of reincarnation.

During the reading, I sit in the back of the room, legs crossed, occasionally looking at my watch. The audience members hug the boy's book to their chests. They cling on to his every word. Amanda holds her copy on her lap. She switches her gaze between the boy and his parents, and at one point I see an almost imperceptible exchange of smiles between her and the boy's father. He, up to this point, has been inanimate.

"It was the Great Depression," the boy says. "The soup my wife made was mostly just watered down chicken stock. Little Sue was our daughter, and she was always crying from hunger. One time, things got so bad we had to eat our pet dog."

"What was the dog's name?" a young child blurts out. The child's mother shushes them and apologizes to the room with a meek smile and the flutter of a hand.

"That's okay," the boy says. "Her name was Tootsie Roll."

I can't help but arch an eyebrow. I enjoy some degree of fantasy, but even this is too hard to believe. I look at my watch again, then at my text messages. A dick pic and a question mark from Jake, who I had saddening sex with once two weeks ago. I save the picture to my phone, delete the text, and check my email. Junk, junk. A forwarded house listing from my mother, who is convinced I'll one day move to the suburbs of Orlando where she lives with her boyfriend and their toy poodle, Cherise. "You need friends," she tells me.

Delete.

"What do your parents think of your past life?" a lone woman asks during Q&A. She has large, brown eyes like a doe. She is wearing a shirt that says BELIEVER in pink and silver sequins.

The boy looks at his parents. I feel myself shiver.

"We are so thankful for our son and his God-given gift," the boy's mother says. The boy's father nods and takes a sip of water. Amanda hurries over to refill his glass.

After the reading and Q&A, there is a brief intermission before the boy is scheduled to sign copies. On my way to the staff restroom, I wonder if the boy even has a signature. It took me so long to develop mine, laboring over lines and lines of my cursive name in my spiral bound notebook.

Lost in thought, I'm surprised when I open the restroom door to find a fully clothed mass heaving, gyrating against the floor's ugly pink tile. The mass turns around and dissipates into two. A sharp little scream emits from the smaller mass, a sound like stepping on a mouse's tail.

Amanda and the boy's father scuttle apart, only there's nowhere for them to scuttle. I stand in the doorway, gazing at this performance. Amanda crawls into the restroom stall and slams the door.

The boy's father turns his back to me, crouching toward the restroom's paper towel dispenser as if he is on time-out. I hesitated for a moment. I hear him fumble with his zipper. I see his chest heaving, his bald spot perspiring, and his brown jeans sagging on his nonexistent ass.

As I close the door to leave, I find that for the first time this evening I am almost gleeful. This, I think, is the realest thing that's happened all night.

The book signing goes off without a hitch and the family prepares to depart. The boy leaves his parents' side and walks over to thank Amanda and I for making the event possible. Amanda's mascara is smudged, and I can't tell if it's from sweat, from tears, or both.

I have a tissue in my pocket that I hand to her. She nods and takes it, wipes the corners of her eyelids.

"Thank you for letting me share my truth in your library," the boy says, staring at me. He puts his hand out and I don't immediately take it.

Amanda smiles at the boy and takes his hand for me, gushing over his words and mannerisms. Despite her smile, she avoids eye contact with his parents, especially his father. To the boy, I offer a tight-lipped nod and bow slightly so as to avoid shaking hands. But I'm unable to avoid touch entirely. Without warning, the boy reaches out and grips me on the shoulder. I can feel each of his fingers against my bone like the talons of a vulture. My jaw clenches. He says, "You look just like my wife from my past life. Her name was Delilah."

I instinctively smack the boy's hand away. It's unintentional, but it's fierce and honest, this violence. Amanda gasps. The boy's parents, who are watching us across the room, shift imperceptibly, but say nothing. The boy puts his hand in his pocket and smirks just like on his book cover.

"Delilah," I say. "How did she die?"

"I don't know," the boy says. "I beat her to it, the dying part."

Weeks later, Amanda forwards me a news article about the boy, his parents, and Once Upon a Time I Was Someone Else. The email's title is "So Sad!!" I'm on my lunch break and eating leftover lasagna. I'm used to Amanda forwarding me junk, and I almost delete the email without reading it.

It turns out that what's in the email is, indeed, sad. The article says that the boy and his parents were recently continuing their literary tour to the Midwest. During an overnight stay in Kansas, a man described as a "stalker" entered the motel room of the family and shot them all, point-blank, dead.

After rereading the scant article, a couple more times, I put down my phone and scrape what's left of the lasagna out of the Tupperware. I find it hard to believe that the boy had a stalker. Who, I wonder, could care that much about another person, let alone a child who made an early fortune from deceit?

I think of Amanda engaged in an impromptu bathroom tryst. A man who is now dead by a shot to the head. What did she see in him? I try to think of his face, but I can't picture it. Only him hunched in the corner of the restroom, kneeling, almost praying to become invisible. The sweat beads on his bald spot gleamed like the scales of a fish.

I also think of the boy with his smirk, his fine-tuned story, his blonde hair matted into a pool of blood. I consider the possibility that he thought he was telling the truth. What then? I snap the lid shut on the Tupperware and close my eyes, imagining what it would be like to believe in something like Amanda and the others. To believe in dying and coming back as someone new, or to believe the others are telling the truth. I think of myself as I am now, faults on faults. I wonder, if reincarnation were real, who I would become next if I could become anyone at all.

Blood and Butter

THE LOCAL NEWS ANCHOR TELLS US about it. A woman was murdered. Afterwards, the killer bit into her throat like a goat devouring a limp stalk of celery. Gratuitous. The scene of the crime, et-cetera. The blood stain looked like an angel sprawled on the cracked pavement. From another angle, it also just looked like blood. On the outskirts of the oxidizing form was a glob of something buttery, yellow, ugly. Sometimes, the dead woman was allowed to contain such things.

One source suggested that the woman was a sex worker. Another suggested that she was a loving mother. That one could be both was left hanging unattended like rotten fruit. Her underwear would be tested for the DNA of strangers and then we would know for sure how to name her ghost.

With hair unwavering, the local news anchor shuffles the papers on his desk. He tells the story with the appropriate degree of regret. His voice curls out of him like an automated parking ticket, like a well-televised serial killer whose neighbors thought was a very nice man.

The Audio Biography of Peter

The neighborhood man invited us over because he said he wanted to show us his VHS collection. Gina thought it would be "fun," and she told me she was planning to interview him with her tape recorder. Gina liked to create what she called "audio biographies". She had a whole box of little tapes on her desk with individual labels like "Mrs. Cat Lady" and "Grampa Joe" and "Mr. Valerio the Mailman". She started making them two summers prior when we turned twelve. She'd get out her tape recorder and hold it next to the person's face and say, "Tell me, Mrs. Garcia, who are you and what are the three most important things about yourself that you want the world to know?" I always admired how brave Gina was. I couldn't even stand looking people in the eyes, and Gina would stand right in front of near-strangers with her handheld recorder and ask them questions I would be too embarrassed to ask in front of a mirror.

The VHS man's name was Peter, and he had lopsided shoulders and freckled hands and a red beard with a streak of white that ran right down the middle. He seemed ancient at the time, which I think now was maybe fifty. He lived one street down from me and Gina and seemed to have no family, no pets, and only piles of gritty dirt and fire ants in his front yard. I didn't tell Gina that I was scared of Peter. I didn't say that I was worried about the way he smiled at kids with his yellow teeth, that I didn't like that he didn't have a dog, and that I didn't care at all about his VHS collection, even if he was willing to let us borrow a few.

But Gina was strong-willed, and I was her shadow. We went to visit Peter on a summer weekday just before dusk. No one knew we were there, which excited Gina and terrified me. The inside of Peter's house smelled like Sharpies and boiled chicken. When I whispered this observation to Gina, she looked at me like I was crazy. With her hands in her jean pockets, she walked around Peter's living room, which did indeed have a large shelf of VHS tapes arranged alphabetically. Peter sat in his armchair with his legs crossed, cracked open a newspaper, and occasionally smiled at us as we perused. Gina ran her fingers over the boxy titles with one hand while her other hand gripped her tape recorder. She didn't look scared or worried, only curious and excited as she read the titles. *The Green Mile, Jerry McGuire, My Girl.*

Peter observed us from over his bifocals. "Are you both movie buffs?" he asked.

"Of course," Gina said. "My favorite movie of all time is Sister Act."

Liar, I thought. Your favorite is *The Blair Witch Project.*

"I have that one if you keep going down the aisle," Peter said. "Whoopi Goldberg, terrific."

It was only when Peter looked at me that I realized I had been staring at him, slack-jawed.

"And you, quiet one? What's your favorite film?"

"Her name's Sarah," Gina said.

Liar.

"Sarah," Peter echoed.

I suddenly had to pee very badly. I didn't like this game that Gina was playing, but I couldn't mentally articulate why. I just knew that I didn't really want to be here, and lying didn't make it any more fun. "Parent Trap," I blurted, which was the truth.

Gina swiveled around and rolled her eyes at me. I knew what she was thinking. You are absolutely no fun.

Peter let out a laugh that sent me into a panic. I clenched my fists.

"What's so funny?" Gina asked.

"Twins are wonderful, just wonderful," Peter said. "You girls are twins, right? It's a very special thing. My sons, they were twins, too."

Were.

I could see the tape recorder rattle in Gina's hand, like she didn't know whether to press record or hide it in her denim pocket. She had not expected Peter to tell us anything personal, at least not before she had the chance to ask. A dead son, this was real. She slid *She's All That* back onto the shelf.

"Unfortunately, one died very young from a rare form of cancer. His name was Thomas. My other son, Matthew, lives with his mother in Tampa. He is seventeen and is a very bright young man. He's going to graduate from high school early. His favorite movie is Mission Impossible. At least it was the last time I asked. I should probably ask again."

No one said anything. What was there to say?

"We are twins," I said. "I'm seven minutes older."

Gina deflated, put out by my baseness, my honesty. She hated that I was older, especially when I didn't seem like it.

"Seven minutes wiser," Peter said and smiled.

Conversation came to a standstill, and all we heard was the whirring of Peter's box fan and the distant barking of a dog.

"Well, I'm sorry about Thomas," Gina finally murmured. She had found *The Craft* and was holding it in her hands with a degree of seriousness, as if holding the Holy Bible and not a thriller about villainous teenage witches.

Peter waived us off. "Life is like that sometimes," is all he said, and brought the newspaper back up to meet his eyes.

I didn't expect how I felt next. All at once, a wave of sadness for Peter and his empty house and his yard full of biting ants came crashing down over me. It appeared that Gina didn't know what to say anymore, that she had suddenly grown too nervous and awkward to ask for an interview. That was a first. I saw her press the tape recorder into her pocket, unsure of what to do next. I thought that at that moment, it was so obvious that we were twins. She looked exactly like me. That is, hopeless.

I felt the primal urge to save her, to save us from whatever this reality was where sickly boys died and their sad dads sat at home in the dark. Fathers whose houses smelled like chemicals and who spent their free time alphabetizing VHS tapes that they had no one to watch with. I licked my chapped lips and sucked in a breath of air. My feet took me to where Gina stood, my hands moist with sweat and shame, and I plucked a random movie from the shelf. I didn't even bother reading the title.

"Can we please borrow this?" I asked. I wasn't ready to look Peter in the eyes, but I did look at his shoes. They were brown and leather and unremarkable. His left foot was turned inward toward his right foot, and it reminded me of the way a toddler holds its body, like it doesn't realize it has one yet and doesn't care what happens to it.

Peter shook his head yes. "You girls can borrow as many as you like. Just do me a favor and rewind them." We promised we would, and soon after that we were gone.

On the walk back home, Gina studied the synopsis on the back of the VHS we'd borrowed and read it aloud in a high-pitched, nasally voice to lighten the mood, though neither of us laughed. It was a movie about a family road trip gone awry. I thought about Peter watching the movie alone at home, sunken into his well-worn armchair, his surviving son and ex-wife far away in Florida. I was still scared of Peter and his yellow teeth, but now I was scared of other worlds, too. I felt small and clumsy in my body, like I was wearing a suit two sizes too large. I thought maybe, somehow, I was drunk. Perhaps it was the overwhelming scent in Peter's house. The acrid smell of Sharpie and boiled chicken. Was that the smell of loneliness? I reached for Gina's hand without thinking, just like when we were little kids, but I missed. Instead, all I grabbed was a handful of the heavy air between us, a hand so strong it clutched and clawed and pulled me to it.

Rind, Peel, and Flesh

AFTER AUNT LUPITA WAS DIAGNOSED with breast cancer, she told me she had a nightmare about a grim reaper with lemon slices for eyes. Not wedges, but circular slices like the kind you find bloating at the bottom of water dispensers in restaurants. I asked what kind of lemons because I didn't know what else to say and she said *Ay, Susie, lemons, just regular lemons, like the kind you get three for a dollar at Albertson's, now let me finish my story, no interruptions, no silly questions to try to lighten up the mood.*

She told me that she believed the nightmare meant that God was giving her an ultimatum: choose to get a mastectomy or choose to die. To Aunt Lupita, the lemons were a symbol for her breasts, which she had always been proud of for their plumpness and heft. I understood the association; my memories of my aunt always involved her giving me a hug, of my face being squished between her enormous chest, which felt more like two overripe cantaloupes than lemons.

She would squeeze my twiggish body between her thick arms and say *Ay, Susie, you are growing into a beautiful young woman.* Eventually, after a few years, I grew taller than Aunt Lupita and instead of my face in her breasts, it was my rib cage to her breasts and she would exclaim *Ay, Susie, if you keep growing, you'll be taller than all the boys, and who's gonna want to marry you, then?*

I couldn't stop growing, though, no matter how much I wanted to one day be loved. And by the time I did actually have a crush on someone—a schoolmate named Luther, a boy with thick-rimmed glasses who gifted me funny drawings in the hallway and always wore a Ramones t-shirt to school—Aunt Lupita's breast cancer diagnosis was the center of my universe and Luther, who I had gone out for ice cream with before he went down on me in the backseat of his car, now felt as intangible as air itself. I hadn't spoken to Luther in nearly two weeks, and I'm pretty sure he thought I wasn't interested in him anymore. He didn't know the truth: I was just scared.

Aunt Lupita said that when she woke up from her grim reaper nightmare, she knew. In order for her to stop the cancer from spreading, she would have to submit to a mastectomy. The next day, I sat next to her on her quilted comforter as she gripped her rosary and called the doctor. Through hot tears, Aunt Lupita agreed to hand her breasts over. Slice, snip. To rid herself of her lemons rind, peel, and flesh.

After the phone call, it was like time moved in slow motion. There was a palpable dread in Aunt Lupita's house when I dropped by to visit after school, and she avoided letting any light in during the day. She began finding clickbait articles on the internet about carcinogens and cancer-fighting root vegetables, and she soon gave up her morning coffee for herbal medicines that she found in sale bins at Albertson's and whose labels she couldn't make sense of.

The doctor scheduled Aunt Lupita's surgery sooner than she had expected. Three days before the mastectomy, she had the grim reaper nightmare again. By that point, I was staying with her almost every night and walking the two miles to school in the mornings. Those walks gave me an opportunity to unravel my worries, to knit them into something else, a fabric that was shoddy and frayed but completely mine. On my walks, I passed the same people at the bus stop holding plastic bags and umbrellas, the same McDonald's employee riding his bike to work, the same tired-looking mom wheeling her infant in the stroller with the janky wheel. The dependability of strangers felt like something I could hold on to, and so I held on tightly.

Aunt Lupita lacked the same kind of security, though. She said that without a man in the house, she felt scared. I guess I was the closest to a man that she had, even though I was a seventeen-year-old junior in high school with back acne and a retainer I wore to sleep every night. My mom worked afternoons as a General Manager at Del Taco, and she had started taking night classes at the local community college in order to get into nursing school. My mom and I hardly saw each other those years, and though I had nothing against her, I sometimes felt like I didn't have a whole lot for her either. In a way, it almost felt like Aunt Lupita was my real parent. She was the one who asked what kind of tea I wanted her to brew up, who told me I needed a shower, who interrogated me about what I wanted to do after I graduated high school.

Mint, please.

I know, I stink.

I have no idea. Something far away from here.

At that, Aunt Lupita always laughed. *Ay, Susie, you remind me so much of myself when I was your age. I always tricked myself into thinking I could escape, find a new boyfriend, get a new job, become famous somehow. But I couldn't escape, and you can't either, no one can. I'm not saying that your life can't be great. I'm just saying that it doesn't matter how smart or beautiful you are. Wherever you go in life, the bad parts of you go too. C'mon, mija, let's pray.*

I appreciated Aunt Lupita's insights, but I hated that they so often ended in a prayer. I didn't believe in God and had stopped going to church in middle school once my mom started working Sundays. As Aunt Lupita prayed, I studied her face: the furrowed lines between the brows, the mole above her lip with the one single hair, the knuckles that bloomed out from her fingers like wooden burls. *Amen.*

Most nights, we sat at Aunt Lupita's dining room table playing dominoes or checkers while she sipped her herbal tea. This night, two nights before her surgery, her mug of tea was full and cold next to her row of dominoes. She was here, yet she was somewhere else too.

"What's the matter?" I asked.

"My stomach." Aunt Lupita said, "The

nerves."

"Can I get you something to eat?" I asked. "Want me to get a bath going?"

"Let's go for a drive," she suggested.

"It's a school night," I said, suddenly feeling old. I cringed, thinking of how I said the same thing to Luther when he tried to take off my jeans. *My hand is cramping from this angle*, he whispered, trying to slide the denim down over my hips. *Well,* I said, grabbing his hand to signal a pause, *it is a school night after all.* At that, he laughed and nodded, pulling his hand away. *10-4.*

"It's only eight p.m., vieja–" Aunt Lupita said. "I'll even let you practice driving."

I couldn't say no to my aunt, so I grabbed her car keys off the counter, and we went. That night, we drove without a destination, mostly down main streets choked with strip malls and shopping centers and parking lots full of cars whose dewy windshields glittered lonesome in the dark. Eventually, Aunt Lupita had me pull into the Walmart parking lot because she said she needed to buy some Jell-o and Campbell's soup for after the surgery, in case all she could do was drink her calories.

"Maybe I'll finally get skinny like you," she joked, pinching my ribs.

In Walmart, we walked through the aisle, and I held Aunt Lupita's basket for her, throwing in whatever boxed or canned items she dictated. Even though there was a cashier working, we went through self-checkout. I asked why. She sighed as she unloaded and scanned her items. *Because I come here all the time—beep—and that cashier is always in a bad mood—beep—and bad energy isn't good for the health of my cells—beep—I read it in an article*, she said. She placed the plastic bags in the crook of my elbows and led the way outside, the bags clanking sharply against my thighs as we walked.

"Have you ever driven on the freeway before?" Aunt Lupita asked as we piled the groceries into the back of the car and slammed the trunk shut.

I told her my mom didn't allow me to drive on the freeway, not until I had a few more months of experience under my belt.

Ay, Susie, let's live a little, she said. *I won't tell your mother.*

So it was decided.

As we drove toward the freeway onramp, Aunt Lupita began rustling through her plastic Walmart bags. She took out a six-pack of chocolate protein shakes, ripped one out of the cardboard holder, and began chugging it as if it were a beer and not an iron-enriched formula for the infirm. She burped loudly, giggled, and sighed.

"Let's listen to some music," she said, and turned on the radio. She flipped through the stations until a rock station came on loud and clear. The Ramones' "Judy is a Punk" was playing, and Aunt Lupita dove right in with an overly singsong rendition.

Jackie is a punk
Judy is a runt
They both went down to Berlin, joined the Ice Capades
And oh, I don't know why
Oh, I don't know why
Perhaps they'll die, oh yeah
Perhaps they'll die, oh yeah

"You know the Ramones?" I asked, stifling a laugh. I couldn't imagine her ever listening to punk rock, only the cheesy Kenny G or the irritating Christian rock she sometimes played while she washed dishes. The most subversive thing I knew my Aunt Lupita to have ever done was the one time she took an avocado off the neighbor's tree without asking. *Ay, Susie, it was hanging on my side of the fence, so it wasn't really stealing*, she'd explained.

"There's a lot you don't know about me, mija. I dated a punk back when I was a little older than you. We even went to see The Ramones play up in San Francisco. We hitchhiked all the way there, can you believe it?"

I didn't reply, instead focusing my eyes on the road. Inside, I reflected on the parallelism of Aunt Lupita and I both having had a crush on a boy who listened to the Ramones. As the car rumbled beneath us, I couldn't shake the feeling that my life was somehow just a dated copy, a bad one at that, and that everything that I'd ever daydreamed about with Luther and beyond had already happened. Except not only had it already happened to Aunt Lupita, and to probably thousands of other girls after that, but it had happened better and more often. That Aunt Lupita was about to have a mastectomy, but maybe I was the one missing out on something.

"How do I merge?" I asked, tapping the

brakes as the car zoomed into the ribbon of sporadic brake lights.

"Just like you're doing, Susie," Aunt Lupita said, closing the plastic cap on her protein shake. We didn't talk for a while after that, and only the sounds of old rock songs made a comment. As we zipped along, I stared straight ahead and maintained exactly 60 mph for what felt like forever, thinking of Aunt Lupita next to me, trying not to think of the way Luther's tongue rooted around hurriedly like he was on an archeological dig. Any car that came up from behind us passed us by. I was glad that Aunt Lupita's car didn't have a bumper sticker like my mom's that said, "STUDENT DRIVER".

"So, where are we going anyway?" I finally asked, peeling my eyes off the road to catch a glance at her.

Only she didn't answer. Aunt Lupita's snores came out of her parted lips light and steady. Her head rested against the seat belt, and for a moment she looked like a baby. A large, old baby with two-inch long gray roots and the remains of chocolate protein shake crusting the edges of her mouth.

Without a response, I was left to come up with one myself. I didn't know where we were going. I didn't know anything, and I was terrified of Aunt Lupita then and of everything she represented. Of what visions she was dreaming up, of her malignant cells multiplying somewhere deep inside of her, of her breasts that sat in her chest like timebombs. The truth was that everything could change in an instant and that, unlike in the movies, it wouldn't always be for the best. I clenched the steering wheel tighter, hating the feeling of being enclosed in this cold metal box.

What if the worst came true? What if Aunt Lupita's dreams actually meant something? And what if she got it all wrong? What if the mastectomy didn't help in the end? That was it, I decided. I wanted to scream, but I didn't, couldn't, so I decided I would do something else instead. I flicked my right blinker on and coasted toward the freeway off ramp. On the way over, I accidentally cut someone off and they honked long and hard to let me know it. Aunt Lupita grunted and shifted in her seat. I waved apologetically and kept going till we were off the interstate, rolling past gas stations and coasting under the full moon above us.

I'd find the way back home. As soon as we got there, I would help Aunt Lupita get to bed and put away her few groceries for her. And in the morning, on my walk to school, I would send Luther a text. I would say that I'm sorry for having disappeared off the face of the earth, but that I was back. I would invite him out into the world, to get a boba after school, to catch a late-night showing of something, anything. Yes, on a school night. I would send the text, and just like life had to be, would always be, I would wait and see what happened.

Duncan

THE YO-YO SLAMS ME IN THE TEETH and I buckle to the ground. It makes the guys gleam to see me on my knees like this, like the women in the videos we watch who are always begging. Tyler grabs his blue jean crotch and says "Nice teats." I am fatter than them, sure. Me and Tyler are thirteen. Ace, fifteen. About my weight, my mom doesn't say that I'm a teenager, that I'm still growing. She says I'll be as fat as my uncle Louis who died from stomach cancer when he was thirty-two. I was too young to remember him. Anytime I open the refrigerator—even for some ice cubes to drop down my shirt in the summer—mom says "It could have been all that sugar that did him in. He didn't eat half as much as you, though."

Where did my tooth go? I try to focus on one thing at a time, ignoring Ace's toady laugh and Tyler saying things we've heard a million times before. "Big ol' titties on Erick," he says, lightly kicking me in the calf. "Did you see how well she took it, that yo-yo in her mouth?" His hands move from his crotch back to the yo-yo. He swings it, winds it up again. Loops and loops around his grubby middle finger. Walk the dog, around-the-world.

"Is the baby crying?" Ace asks, standing over me.

"It sthucking hurths," I say. I managed to get up on one knee.

"It was an accident," Tyler says, not looking at me.

"But it sure made me hard," Ace says. He looks at Tyler for approval.

Tyler doesn't respond, keeps working the yo-yo like a marionette doll. We're behind the old Pizza Hut where we go to poke at condom wrappers, half-empty cans of beer, lone tufts of black hair. I half-heartedly look for the tooth, my hand mumbling over gunky bottle caps and dried balls of chewing gum.

When I find it, a shiny yellow-white fleck nestled atop a piece of potato chip bag, Tyler is rocking the baby. His face is calm, a sheet of pale dough. Paternal, almost. Maybe this is what Louis looked like. I don't know anything about him aside from the fact that he was my uncle, and he was fat like I am, and he had cancer. Maybe he was like Tyler somehow. Maybe it's good that he's dead. I dust the tooth off and stuff it deep in the front pocket of my t-shirt.

"You do a trick," Tyler says, throwing the yo-yo at me.

The yo-yo feels heavy in my hand, my jaw throbbing with pain. The only thing I'm able to do is make the yo-yo sleep. It purrs on the ground near the rest of my blood.

Tyler stomps it, grabs his crotch. "That one is called 'gang bang,'" he says.

"Gang bang," Ace says. He laughs and also grabs his crotch. They both look at me.

"Gang bang," I say. I grab my crotch. When I pull my hand away, the splayed, bloody fingerprints look like pitiful stains. Like a person turned upside-down and falling.

Before We All Go Under

OLLIE IS AT IT WITH CHARCOAL AGAIN, not so much drawing as gouging into the paper. Scraping the sharp contours of the face, the angled jaw and cavernous chin. They are drawing a picture of their father, his body all dressed up in a suit and tie and his hands folded neatly over his paunchy stomach. The charcoal carves his pockmarked cheekbones into being, and the notepad makes sharp little scratchy sounds as its heap of pages flap with their movements. I don't think this is appropriate at an open casket–Ollie drawing, me watching them draw, me judging them for being fifteen, for being profoundly sad and awkward in a way I don't want to remember.

Sometimes I feel that as I age, I am becoming austere and Victorian in an invisible and dangerous way. The older I get, the more distant from people like Ollie I feel, the more alien. Sometimes I think it is at odds with my appearance. Septum ring, eyebrows bleached, the bluebird tattoo huddled against the nest of my ribcage, beak open to the dark mole beneath my left breast. *There's a bluebird in my heart that wants to get out, but I'm too tough for him.* When I was young I used to read Bukowski, I used to go on road trips to Hollywood at 2 a.m. on a school night, I used to chain smoke at the drive-in with whoever I was dating that month, that week. And before then, I used to cut myself in between my toes with an X-Acto knife so that I'd always feel the pain wherever I walked. For a while, Ollie–when they were known as Olivia–used to think I was the cool aunt. I wore a leather jacket, and my nail polish was always chipped. They didn't know that I was just sad. Maybe I'm still sad. These days I rub Vaseline on my heels before bed and scroll on my phone till I don't remember who I am, how I got here, or what I want.

In some ways I would like to ignore Ollie altogether, to be the kind of person who doesn't notice a child drawing instead of crying at their father's funeral. Wouldn't that be so easy? If only I could be the kind of person who solemnly conducts customs without obtrusive internal monologues and second-guesses. But here I am, and I can't stop watching Ollie drag the charcoal nub across the wrinkly sheet. Such concentration, such fury. Their fingertips are little tense fires, flickering pink and white and black. I feel inexplicably proud of them.

I wonder if Ollie wonders what other people think of them. Self-consciousness in the teenage way, but also the human way. I wonder if they know that even though they are their own person, I can't help but see their father, his mannerisms, his thick brown eyebrows that formed little question marks over his stormy irises. Sometimes I want to call Ollie "Jim". Ollie holds the charcoal like my brother Jim used to hold his pencils while my mom helped him with his algebra homework—that is to say, incorrectly and too close to the paper so as to cause smears. I miss him, my brother, and I miss the simple lives we used to have. The life, period. Hearts beating. I peer over Ollie's shoulder. The portrait is flat and dense and true of a corpse who even before death spent years deflating with sickness.

When Ollie is done drawing, they turn toward me. For approval? For a word of encouragement? I was never good at reading teenagers, not even when I was one myself. I tilt my head and attempt a smile, but I think it manifests as an awkward grimace. They slap their notepad shut and move away from me toward the refreshments table. I say "Sorry,

Ollie," under my breath, but they don't hear me, and even if they did, what would be the point of responding to your aunt with the bleached eyebrows and the words stuck in her throat like a broken cork in a bottle of wine?

Water, coffee, tea. There's nothing sweet for children at the refreshments table. I watch Ollie pretend to want a cup of ice and then slosh it around in the cup with their blackened finger. For the rest of the service, they don't look at their dead father, their mother shrunken with grief, their cousins, or the line of other distant relatives and acquaintances lined up to say farewell to Jim.

Father. Husband. Son. Brother. Stardust.

Sometimes I wish I could do the things my heart tells me to do. I would like to be softer, a gum eraser between a budding artist's fingers. A good aunt and a better person. I would like to be the kind of human who might alleviate pain, who might be a safe place for someone who doesn't have one. I would like to learn how to reach out to a heavy shoulder and touch it. How wonderful would that be? To have words to fill the silence and make it a song.

Tender Hoof

THINGS ARE DIFFERENT NOW, DEADER. In the past, we used to turn the cow into the leather sofa while the cow was still alive. Those were purer times. The 1990s. It was normal to sit on the couch to watch a scary movie with the neighbor, sneaking handholds in the dark, while the tanned and scrunched face rustled faintly behind us.

It wasn't uncommon for people to name their couches. They became pets, in a way. Still, my mom didn't like the idea of a name; the cows tended to die right when your body's imprint was starting to take shape on the grunting stretch of bovine. At the point when the cushions became cracked and soft, the entire couch had to be left out on the sidewalk for the city's trashmen. From my bedroom window, I watched them haul the couches off while they smoked and joked about a passing runner's body. Sometimes they even burnt the couches with their cigarettes and laughed. Roast beef, they said.

As if the couches were edible, which they

weren't. As if that would have stopped some people from trying anyway.

Of course, I knew what was wrong with all of this. The cows were lonely. I almost never sat on our couch after I started my sophomore year in high school, got a part-time job at a dying video store, and started dating a boy called Ziggy. It was also that weird, crossover time in the late 1990s when leather couches made of dead cows first debuted. I remember going over to my friend Sarah's house one day after school. It was our senior year of high school. Her parents were doctors and never home. But what a home. The house was a museum of tasteful vases and arching rows of CDs and a refrigerator full of Perrier. When I asked Sarah why her couch was dead, where its tail was, she sipped on a Perrier, looked at me and said, "I won't sit on anything with a face."

How unfortunate for the old couches to be abandoned in this way. As if they'd never existed, all that pain and work. I even began to sit on them less and less. And then I went away to college, my body newly relegated to the corners of library floors, my dorm room's papasan chair, the cool concrete staircase leading up to the university's study hall.

But I did come home for the summer and

spring breaks. My parents were one of the only houses left in our neighborhood that still had a living couch. It was like sitting in a barn full of musty memories. The dust floated around my face and stuck to my sweaty skin in a shivering sheet.

One summer, after driving home from my junior year in college, I arrived at my parents' house, which was at the end of a cul-de-sac. It reminded me of those warm suburban nights that I used to hate but had since grown to miss. Those nights had a shadow to them that my dorm room couldn't conjure, even with a black light. A unique and ancient sadness, like the time I discovered a nest with punched-out eggs in my family's kitchen trash can. The whole mass was covered in ketchup. Who would do such a thing? No one had an answer. We never had ketchup in the refrigerator, or enough patience for slow cruelty.

I grabbed my backpack from my car and slipped inside the still house. Mom and dad were already in bed, I guessed. I dropped the backpack on the floor of the living room, sat on the couch—which was quite old by then—and held its tender hoof. It was like cradling an old photo album filled not only with dead people, but with dead people who were saying, "Why should I be dead? You should be dead, too." And the only way to answer was to cover their eyes with your thumb, to pretend you deserved to be here.

Something I Will Never Tell You

THE ICE MAN LOVES ME MOST when I am almost dead. Every Thursday afternoon we meet at the Pelican Ice freezer for the usual two bags of ice, and then we go inside the gas station shop for some snacks. The Ice Man wants me dead, but he doesn't want me hungry. I usually choose a sleeve of powdered donuts off the rack, the kind that leaves a sugary snow everywhere they go. The Ice Man picks up a pack of spearmint gum for himself and pays for the purchase with a crisp twenty dollar bill pulled from a silver money clip. We meet in my part of town, and my part of town is far enough from his part of town that he doesn't have to think twice about who he'll see or who will see him.

Do you remember how much I enjoyed reading when I was growing up? I still love to read, but these days I never seem to be able to find the time to pick up a book. Sometimes the stories I tell myself while riding the bus to work and back are enough, but sometimes not. In the bedroom I rent that you'll never set foot in, I have a bookshelf full of secondhand spines, mostly paperbacks from thrift stores. Fantasy, sci-fi, romance. My favorites are any used books that have someone else's name handwritten inside their front covers. In a way, finding someone's handwritten name like that feels like opening up a love letter, like being desired.

My to-read list is so big that I don't even need a nightstand. I just pile the books next to my mattress and set my candle on top of the stack along with my coffee mug and ashtray. I started smoking about two years ago just to see. I'm still seeing. Maybe it's not safe, the flammable things next to the flames, but I'm okay with that. Despite everything I'll never tell you, I consider myself a very careful person.

You know that I've had large breasts since 7th grade because you were the one who cursed at me every time one of my thick bra straps tangled up in the washing machine at the laundromat and strangled one of your work shirts to hell. Even though my breasts meant nothing to me other than inconvenience, they seemed to be the source of almost every momentous life event from then forward. And maybe you didn't know that, but did you know that for the most part I hate having breasts at all? Before I met the Ice

Man, I used to wear compression bras that squashed my torso into a firm lump and made me feel finally put-together, tidy, inside the lines of myself. Maybe you don't eat Spam anymore like we used to but think of my body like that canned block of meat. I craved an existence that was compact, ultra-processed, and orderly. Everything is all there just like you would expect and anything that could go wrong has already gone wrong and is now neatly cubed.

Another thing I will never tell you is that I met the Ice Man because I responded to an ad on the internet. I know you always warned me about that kind of thing. I know what you would call someone like me behind my back, but I don't even get paid. And while it's true that I don't have money, this one thing in my life isn't about the money. It's about something else entirely, something that lives knotted between my ribs. Something that I would never tell you about, and something about which you would never think to ask.

I wouldn't say that meeting the Ice Man has changed my life, but it has made me feel different about myself in a way that's hard to explain. It's kind of like opening your eyes when it's pitch dark and expecting to see. That kind of disorienting experience is also a magical one, like being turned inside-out. I feel naked around the Ice Man most of the time, even when I'm clothed. It's like he can see right through me, but I also feel unashamed. All there are shards of ice clinking together in bath water and his body straddled against me like a climber mounting Mt. Everest, his dick the pickaxe. How minute and inconsequential his sex is against a snowy mountain like me.

You would never ask, and I would never tell you the details. The Ice Man fills the bath with cold water. Then we pour in the ice together but don't say anything. It's like that because even though we have this act in common, we don't have other things in common like spouses, children, mortgages, or 401ks. We're in it together, but we're also in our own heads. Sometimes the Ice Man whistles aimlessly to himself and answers text messages from his wife on his smartwatch. There is no foreplay involved, or this is the foreplay. Sometimes I suck on an ice cube and run my fingers through the running water in preparation. One time, his wife called the Ice Man's cell phone during the time we were filling the tub and he had to take it, so I put the ice in by myself and waited as I heard his muffled voice through the walls.

"Are you taking a bath?" I heard the wife ask, incredulous, as he exited the room.

"I'm giving the dog a bath," the Ice Man said, feigning a sigh. "She rolled in shit. Again."

It's pretty much the same every time once the ice bath is ready. When he comes back to the bathroom, the Ice Man smiles at me cheerfully, unwraps his pack of gum, and sticks a piece in his mouth. This part is cordial and fleeting, like passing a stranger on the sidewalk and giving them a friendly nod. You're a human and I'm a human, isn't that nice? The Ice Man takes a seat on the toilet and observes what I do next. I sink into the tub up to my chin for five minutes and pretend to die. In the ice water, my breasts float above me as pellets of ice tap, tap, tap against them.

It's the coldest I've ever been. A part of me dies, but it's the part I wouldn't miss anyway.

After five minutes, the Ice Man helps pull me out of the water and lays me on a thick beach towel pre-positioned next to the tub. The warmth of the air temperature and his body heat makes my skin prickle and sear. My eyes are closed, mouth open in a dramatically dead way, sort of like a fish laid out on a bed of ice at the seafood counter. The Ice Man checks to make sure I'm dead. His fingers pressed against my neck are hot sticks of dynamite. I hold my breath. I hear the metal clamor of his belt. As he touches me, I can feel his skin light up with goosebumps. A minute passes. I think I can hear his toes curl against the terry bath mat. My feet are on fire with warmth and feeling, and I try not to let my teeth chatter because that's not what I agreed to, and I have a part to play. We both do.

After we're done, he leaves the guest bathroom to take a hot shower alone in the main bathroom and I take a hot shower alone in the guest bathroom. Afterwards, I engulf myself in guest towels and blankets to warm me back to life. I try to heat up my fingers enough to clumsily tear into the sleeve of donuts. The powder gets everywhere, all over my breasts, in the corners of my mouth, in my wet braids, such a mess but also weightless.

I have to think that the Ice Man's wife doesn't get cold and dead for him. Why would she? She doesn't need a part to play because she's already part of something big: his life. They have two children together. I've seen the kids in hallway picture frames looking simple and happy. I wonder how The Ice Man handles his wife's warmth. I imagine him crawling into bed with her most nights, and I think that their bodies must turn into a small fleshy fire under the duvet. I wonder if a small part of him–or maybe a large part of him–resents her and her heat, her aliveness, her telling him that he's taking up too much of the bed, cursing that his alarm ringtone is starting to annoy the fuck out of her morning after morning, year after year. I wonder if they love each other, or when they stopped loving each other. I wonder what that's like.

On the rare occasions when you and I speak on the phone, you give me a hard time for not telling you any details. It's true that I'm tight-lipped, but only because I don't think you'd like the details. The dead-end jobs, the credit card debt, the one guy I dated for two weeks who ghosted me after drunkenly observing that the cellulite on my ass looked like moon craters. You and I are not friends, we are family. I could never tell you that even after he ghosted me, I texted him asking if he wanted to come over, that I thought I loved him. He never responded, and I stopped texting, but I never deleted his phone number.

Sometimes it feels like I'm outside of myself watching my life unfold. Once, when the Ice Man was on top of me, I opened my eyes just for a moment. It was off script, but I had zoned out and forgot I was supposed to be acting like a corpse. I was surprised to find that the Ice Man was closing his eyes too, not even looking at the frosty dead girl in front of him. One of his hands was wrapped around his dick and the other was pressed against my rib cage, which I could hardly feel at all except for the pressure of his weight.

It was from this vantage point that I really saw the lines in his face, the cracks in his lips. He was old, I realized. At least twenty years my senior. His mouth was pursed into a dry little bouquet, and I thought he looked absolutely deceased. I had to stifle a laugh, and I closed my eyes again. I thought about you then, isn't that weird? I would absolutely never tell you that, because I would have to tell you so much else. But I thought about what you were doing right then at that moment, and I hoped it was something that made you feel good.

And though I usually don't call you, I thought at that moment that I would give you a call when I got home, sometime after I towel-dried my braids, turned the bathtub faucet to HOT, and watched the last of the ice cubes melt down the drain. I had the urge to tell you how great things were and to make you feel proud. I wanted to give you details for once, something that would make you feel like you'd done something right in raising me. I am always so ready to lie. I will lie to make you remember to love me, and I will lie down and get cold if that's what it takes to be touched. I can be the freezing mountain, or I can be the cratered moon that looms above it. I'll never ask you "What do you want me to be?" But whatever it is, I can try. I can float in the bathtub and hold my breath and pray my lips turn blue. Play dead. I can wait patiently for an embrace if it takes my whole life, flesh frozen as solid ice, bones at the ready.

Bell

I DON'T HAVE A SOUND unless someone gives me a sound, knocks me around.

A bedridden child used to knock me around often. She rang me for water, rang me when she wanted the shutters turned askew. She needed to watch her older sister meander in the garden with her drawing pad, needed to watch her flirt with the neighbor boy who was supposed to be hers, needed to hate her and wish she were dead. She told me so. Or else she told the drapes, or the doorknob, or God, whoever. It doesn't matter. It must have been soothing to consider the possibility of an aching death that was not her own.

For five or six days each month, she rang me when she needed her menstrual dressing changed. Rang me when she was spiteful and bored, rocking me so that my tongue gouged the roof of my mouth. She rang me in sync with her rattling breath and her phlegm-filled coughs. She rang me when she thought she was going to die, once and for all.

One day, she did die. She neglected to ring

me at that time. She made her own garbled song with coughing and gasping. The parents huddled around her body and patted her forehead with a damp cloth. The older sister sat in a far corner of the room. So did the boy who was supposed to belong to the dying girl. He let the sister cry into his shoulder, let her blow mucus into his blue linen handkerchief.

After the girl's body was removed and her funeral service was held, the sister returned with the boy to the bedroom where her sister had died. I was gathering dust on the nightstand. Dead skin from the dead girl. My tongue hadn't flapped in over a week. The girl led the boy to the bed. She picked me up and rang me, as if it were the first time she'd ever seen me. Upon hearing my music, their faces seemed to age. They got undressed and he tried touching her where he thought it might be pleasurable. The girl's face was blank as he jabbed at her with his fingers. When she told him to stop, he seemed relieved. She straddled him on the same sheets her sister had died on. Their sex was soundless, their pale bodies thumping against each other as if hollow. "I'm coming," she finally whispered into his ear. "Really?" the boy asked. "It's possible," she replied. They moved their bodies some more and when he came on her thigh, she got dressed at once. Not even bothering to wipe herself, she told him he should go.

He went.

Soon thereafter, everything changed. My tongue was removed by the dead child's mother. It was placed into a tiny velvet pouch and stuffed back inside of me. It reminded me of something I'd seen the dying child do to her dolls at night after she'd stripped them of their lace dresses. This was before she got truly sick. I was packed into a box with other odds and ends and given to someone new. They displayed me on a shelf in a thrift store for seven years. I was paired with emerald brooches and metal, star-shaped buttons. Someone finally bought me for much less than I was worth. An older woman who had just the right place for me.

Now I live on a small wooden shelf filled with other bells, some older, some younger, some larger, some smaller. My tongue was reinstated. Some people call them clappers, which isn't right at all. They are our tongues. Some people wink and say our tongues go ring-a-ding-ding. To me it feels more like oh-no-no-no, like something fleshy inside of me that scares me to think about it for too long. Perhaps it's like having only a trachea, or a sphincter, or a heart. And yet, no one rings me much anymore except to test me. They want to see if I still work. In fact, I do. When they pick me up, I get to show them that after everything, I still have something worth listening to.

Crumbs

A WEEK BEFORE ANNA PLANNED TO DIE, we stood in my kitchen making eggplant parmigiana. She'd already divulged her morbid desire to me days prior, certain I would keep her secret. For some reason, I did; we were two eggs whisked. I thought our dinner date would change her mind—the smell of eggplant crisping in olive oil, Pavarotti exploding on the record player, Limoncello in old jam jars. What about this life wasn't to love? I laid a red-and-white checkered cloth on the table. Anna smirked as I complained about the lumps of egg and breadcrumbs in between my fingers. I watched her pale hands as she patted the excess grease off the gold medallions of eggplant, Anna herself a treasure. I pulled one of her greasy hands to my face and kissed it on the knuckles. Those knuckles were cold. Anna made the joke about the warm heart and smiled, pulled her hand away.

At Anna's funeral, everyone brought food. Nieces with bruschetta, aunts with penne arabiatta, an estranged uncle with frutti de mari. The clams stank in the hot sun. Anna's family mourned at her casket and ate after the burial, right there in the grass next to the six-foot-deep hole and the two-foot tall photo of Anna when she was still a child, when she was still a Catholic. Grandmas sat next to the hole on lawn chairs, crying with spaghetti sauce on their chins. Young cousins fought over pizza, too confused about death to really think about it. Parents toothed the edges of their blue Solo cups. Even the priest had a plate. Though not family, not even Italian or Italian-American, I ate right along with all of Anna's relatives. No one asked who I was, and I was too upset to speak, certain we were all there because of what I had done, which was nothing.

Roma tomatoes, fresh linguine, garlic marinara, spicy meatballs. The smell of freshly-turned earth was a seasoning no one wanted, but it had infiltrated everything, even the cheesy armor of the ziti. And once it was in, it was in.

Goodbye, Goodbye

I HATE MAGIC AND SO SHOULD YOU. Without knowing it, you can contract it from taking a sip out of someone else's water bottle, or touching a sticky handle, or reaching underneath the refrigerator into the gritty unknown. First, an itchy throat. Then vomiting, nausea, and lying next to the toilet's base with your head wrapped in a milky caul of stabbing stars. And after you throw it up you have to eat it. The fucked up rules of magic. It's worse than having a period. You'll see it when you're older. Magic always gets caught in your teeth, even when you try to slurp it. But when you try to swallow magic, it turns to chalk. And if you try to savor magic, it dissolves into a bland oil the exact temperature of your boredom. Eventually, it goes down.

To some people magic tastes like metallic playground equipment, the rusty chain of an abandoned swing set. To others it tastes like canned apricots. What do you think it tastes like, sister? I think it tastes like nightmares in the shape of sadness and smallness. Like the time you and I got lost in the supermarket. We let go of Mom's hand to get a better look at a stranger's face. Didn't you hate that too, all that magical wonder? How magical it was to be alone for the first time, crawling into corners and touching the beige shoes of women with spines curved like hilltops. Our throats began tingling. We huddled together by the toaster strudels. It was too cold there in the freezer aisle. We waited to be found, waited for the magic of Mom, but it turned out that no one was looking for us. Mom had already left, forgetting about us completely. You vomited first, magic on the linoleum. I tasted it with my pinky finger. Then you pointed to the window. Do you remember now? Outside, the sky was magical. So terrifying. I didn't want to look, but I did anyway. The clouds had already turned splendid with stars forming at their edges, like hands opening and closing and waving to the enormity of our little childhood: goodbye, goodbye.

The Man Before Her

I WATCHED THE MAN AND HIS WIFE in aisle four: tea, coffee, and cereal. I saw it happen. I was there with my daughter, Maribel, when she was almost two. All that blood. It was a lot to live through. It still is.

Maribel loved going to the grocery store back then. The music, the lights, the rickety metal carts with plastic child seats that were cool against her chubby legs. She squealed at the sensation, and I called her Screech Owl, My Little Screech Peach, leaning in close to smell the baby drool in her clothes.

And I'm glad she enjoyed those trips so much, because a big part of me hated them, dreaded them. I was hurt. Maribel's mother should have been there with us deciding which brand of orange juice to buy, but instead she was all the way in California. She left us shortly after Maribel was born after saying she wasn't ready for a family at nineteen. So, she drove home to Santa Barbara, back to her parent's house, and that was that. Sometimes she sent money, but she didn't want to talk to me on the phone or hear Maribel's changing voice. She never said it directly, but I know she was thinking: What was the point?

One time, when Maribel was four, I went on a date with a woman named Diane at a sandwich shop. She asked about Maribel's mom, and I said she had left us, but that there wasn't really a reason why. She just hadn't wanted to be a parent. Diane gave me a confused look, sipped her root beer. I could tell she didn't believe me, didn't believe that could possibly be all it was. That it had to be something about me, the man sitting before her. I could see her stirring in the silent questions as she twirled her straw and studied the bacon in her BLT. Was I abusive? Was my penis grotesque? Was I an idiot? She had been polite after that, if a little reserved, and she didn't return my voicemail asking for a second date.

To tell the truth, I didn't really want a second date, or not with Diane anyway. But that's the kind of person I am. I knew Diane wouldn't want to meet me again, so I called her. I pursued her rejection. She delivered it in the form of silence, and it was just the answer I needed. I continued with my solitary, single dad life with Maribel, who by then was about to start school.

And maybe it really was something about me. But what could I do? What was more traumatic, our abandonment from Maribel's mother or that day in the grocery store? I think all that tragedy is so much for a toddler, for anyone, even a father. But Maribel says she doesn't remember it anyway. She's twenty-two now. She's headstrong, my Screech Owl, studying medicine and dating a kid named Roger. He's a book smart but dull junior who aspires to be a lawyer and only wears white socks. Maribel thinks she'll marry him. I think he doesn't know how to hold a real conversation or push his chair back in. How will he make my daughter happy? Does it require that little? Have I been trying too hard all these years?

Whenever I bring up that terrible incident in the grocery store all those years ago, Maribel shrugs, rolls her eyes.

"I don't remember any of it, Dad. I only remember you talking about it," she says, before going back to her phone, scrolling, smirking at something that Roger sent her.

And we were scrolling, rolling down aisle four looking for Cheerios. Maribel loved to crush the brittle rings in her little fists, to throw them at me, to chew them into mash and spit them back out. It was when I was grabbing for the box off the shelf when the man entered the aisle from the other end. He was a handsome enough guy, late twenties with curly brown hair and a corduroy jacket, only a little out of place because he didn't have a cart, or a basket and his arms were empty.

That was an unusual sight in the grocery store. A man without a wife, without a child, without anything in his hands. At least I had Maribel to tote around. Her presence protected me as much as mine protected her.

But then, the man did have something in his hands. A lump in his corduroy jacket. Out came a handgun. It happened so quickly, I didn't have time to react. He said the woman's name loud and clear: "Mary." Just as Mary was turning toward him, he shot. He didn't miss. Mary's husband dropped his box of oatmeal. The man shot the husband, too. His aim was right. I picked Maribel up out of the cart, and we ran to Produce. It was only a few aisles away.

Another shot fired. Shoppers screamed, scattered, plunged.

Everything after that was a blur, and I didn't know what to do. We made it to Produce, but we were toward the back of the store, not near the store entrance. Maribel and

I hid behind a display of berries. Blueberries, blackberries, and raspberries were all on sale. Maribel seemed mildly inconvenienced at all the commotion, a sort of fake cry spreading across her face. With trembling hands, I grabbed a container of raspberries–Maribel's favorite–and gave her a handful to snack on. She smiled, ate them, and puckered.

"Sour," she said.

"Sour," I agreed.

It was a big news story that week, that month, that year. Small town murder-suicide. Love triangle. Everyone died. And that's where I end the story when I tell it to Maribel, which isn't as often these days. I don't tell her that I almost fainted that day in the grocery store, that I pissed myself and that the police officers pretended not to notice the smell when they took down my witness statement. That I had to pull over on the drive home so that I could vomit onto the hot pavement and that it splattered back onto my piss-soaked denim jeans. I don't tell her how ashamed I am for being the kind of person who hides behind a display of fruit when disaster strikes, that even today I am woefully unprepared for the worst.

I also don't tell Maribel that sometimes I still think of her mother, and I feel a rage and loneliness so deep that it feels like I'm a hollowed-out gourd. I don't tell her that I'm simultaneously enraged at Lisa, but also jealous. To not want to be a parent, or a wife, to be free and to not really care. I envy that disconnect.

I don't tell Maribel that I found Lisa on Facebook recently either, and that she is listed as "In A Relationship" and living in Reno. I don't throw down my phone and say, "What the fuck could she possibly be doing in Reno, Nevada?" Instead, I study Lisa's profile closely. In her profile picture, her once-brown pixie cut is a flowing jet black. She's leaning against the railing to the Grand Canyon, "In A Relationship" probably taking her photo. She always said she wanted to travel.

I don't tell Maribel that her mother looks happy.

And I would never tell Maribel the most shameful part of all, that for a brief second before the man in the corduroy jacket became violent, I felt a sense of recognition. At that moment I thought, *He looks like me. I have a jacket just like that.* I thought, *A single man, a kinship.*

No, none of that passes my lips. I only tell Maribel that I love her, and it's perfectly alright that she doesn't remember that day in the grocery store, that it's nothing to worry about. That it's just a Dad thing, all the broken record stories, and I'll finally stop talking about it once and for all. That it really wasn't anything worth remembering.

Hatched

LILY AGREED TO HAVE DINNER WITH ME in my car. She wanted to see how I lived, and I wanted to see if she could handle it. When she arrived, I was checking my eyeliner in the rear view mirror. She knocked on the passenger's side window with the blunt edges of her painted fingernails. In the crook of her arm was a wooden bowl covered in plastic cling wrap. I unlocked the doors, reached across the passenger's seat, and let her in.

"I love hatchbacks," she said, placing the bowl on top of the dashboard. "I used to have one for a while in college."

"It's surprisingly comfortable to sleep in," I said.

"I slept in mine a couple times. Too wasted to drive home after parties, I think. If I'm remembering correctly," she continued, "I wouldn't describe it as 'comfortable'".

"Fair," I said.

Lily poked me in the arm. She wanted me to lighten up.

"Is that salad?" I asked, pointing to her

wooden bowl.

"Greek," she said.

"Great. I'll put some music on," I said, and reached for my phone with sweaty hands. I scrolled aimlessly, unsure of what Lily would want to listen to. Superficially, she seemed much different than me. She was nine years my senior, grew up in Ohio, and worked as a graphic designer. I knew nothing about Ohio or graphic design. I met her at a coffee shop three weeks ago. Unlike me, Lily was an oversharer. She told me she'd dated lots of women throughout her life, but also some men. She'd given a baby up for adoption when she was still in college. Said she still thought a lot about the child, who was now a teenager living somewhere in Minnesota.

"Where do you keep all your stuff?" she asked. She shifted her body to peer into the backseat. All that was there was a Tupperware container filled with paper plates, plastic spoons, and plastic cups. She seemed to expect piles of clothing, books, toiletries. The sorts of things that make people human.

"In the back," I said. Then, acknowledging my half-lie, I continued, "Also, under the car. Well, when I have guests. There's a lot of clutter, otherwise."

She smiled. "And what's for dinner?" she

asked.

I observed her smile. It reminded me of my mother's mouth when she also sat in the passenger's seat—cracked and drained of life. Part of Lily's discomfort, I knew, was her frustration with my reticence. I hadn't told her what college was like, wasn't eager to share anything about exes or family or traumatic experiences. These things didn't make me feel any closer to people. In fact, they made me feel more alone than ever.

"Macaroni and cheese," I said.

"How do you make that in a car?" Lily asked.

"I make it outside on a camping stove," I said. "It's easy when it's not windy."

"Wow," she said.

"Yes," I said. I opened my car door, walked to the back seat, and removed the bowl of macaroni and cheese.

"Do you have tongs?" Lily asked, watching me. "Something to serve the salad? I forgot to bring anything."

I looked at Lily and she looked at me. Her eyes seemed to narrow, harden, shrink.

"I think I have something under the car," I said. "But it's under the car."

"We can look," she said.

"No, you don't have to—" I started.

"To what?" Lily asked.

"You know what I mean," I said.

"I don't," she said.

"The car. Everything," I said.

"I mean, we can look," she said, opening the passenger side door.

I placed the macaroni and cheese on the dashboard. Outside, Lily was already on her hands and knees, pulling Tupperware containers out from beneath us. A duet of scraping and sighs as she maneuvered around on the cold ground. Lily wasn't even close to where a pair of tongs would be. I told her so. But she continued. She was in a box of socks and underwear, in a small bag of knitting yarn, in a Ziploc baggie of egg remnants from the one chick I'd seen hatch on my grandfather's farm. Then she was reaching into a cookie tin filled with photos of old lovers. She pulled out a polaroid photo of breasts I hadn't seen in person in three years, tossed it aside.

"Stop—" I said.

But she didn't stop. Next were my lucky coins, my childhood stamp collection, a series of state-themed magnets for the fantasy version of myself that owned a house with a kitchen and a refrigerator. Then another bin: my dead dog's collar, expired acne prescriptions, a vibrator the shape and color of a skyscraper. She tried to turn it on, but the batteries were dead. And still further, an older container: one box of journals from the past ten years, a suicide note no one but me had ever read, a stack of therapist's business cards with numbers I'd never called, and so on. She scanned the letter, nodded, and placed it aside. Kept digging.

I shivered and got back in the car. I could see Lily's calves and shoes protruding from beneath me. I pressed the car horn. She sprang up, dusted herself off, put her hands up as if to say, "What gives?"

But my foot was already heavy on the gas pedal by then. The sound of crunching over boxes filled with trinkets and paper. In a brief moment of regret, I glanced at Lily's form in the rearview mirror. She had found the tongs after all. She was already using them to sift through what little remained of me.

Acknowledgments

"Demolished" appeared in *The Cincinnati Review: MiCRo Series*

"Crumbs" appeared in *The Cincinnati Review: MiCRo Series* & the *Best Microfiction 2019*

"Don't Mention It" appeared in *Newfound Magazine*

"Duncan" appeared in *Cleaver Magazine*

"Hatched" appeared in *SmokeLong Quarterly* and was anthologized in *Flash Fiction America*

"Tender Hoof" appeared in *Longleaf Review*

In addition to these publications, the author extends a huge thank you to the critique group at Western Colorado Writers' Forum for providing invaluable insight and encouragement to these stories.

About the Author

Nicole Rivas is the author of TENDER HOOF: STORIES (Thirty West Publishing, 2024) and the flash fiction chapbook A BRIGHT AND PLEADING DAGGER (Rose Metal Press, 2018). Her stories have been published in journals such as *Longleaf Review, SmokeLong Quarterly,* and *The Cincinnati Review,* and her flash fiction has been anthologized in Best Microfiction (2019), The Best Small Fictions (2019), and W.W. Norton's Flash Fiction America (2023). www.nicolemrivas.com

About the Publisher

Follow us on:

Scan the QR code to visit www.thirtywestph.com

www.ingramcontent.com/pod-product-compliance
Lightning Source LLC
Chambersburg PA
CBHW031548310726

48971CB00008B/2674